UG-A-LUG

FOUR CAVEMEN AND A PREHISTORIC PENCIL

For Rosie and Alistair,
Jack and Charlotte – JL

WRITTEN BY **JILL LEWIS**

For Erin and Isla – SR

ILLUSTRATED BY **SIMON RICKERTY**

SIMON AND SCHUSTER
First published in Great Britain in 2014
by Simon and Schuster UK Ltd
1st Floor, 222 Gray's Inn Road,
London WC1X 8HB
A CBS Company

978-1-4711-1728-2 (HB)
978-1-4711-1729-9 (PB)
978-1-4711-1730-5 (eBook)
Printed in China
10 9 8 7 6 5 4 3 2 1

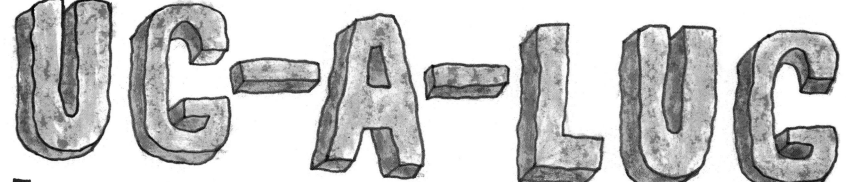

UG-A-LUG

FOUR CAVEMEN AND A PREHISTORIC PENCIL

SIMON AND SCHUSTER
London   New York   Sydney   Toronto   New Delhi

A little boy loved drawing.
He loved drawing cavemen best of all.
If only they were real!
What fantastic adventures they could have.

Colin

Clive

The little boy went to get a drink.
As he left, he accidentally knocked
over his pot of pencils and . . .

. . . something amazing happened!

Carlos

Flint

THUD!

A pencil rolled over the cavemen's fire – and put it out!

The picture had come to life!

'Ug-a-loof?!' said Carlos, pointing at the pencil.

'DOOF!' said Flint.

He was cross. That fire had taken three days to get going!

The cavemen wondered what to do with the pencil.

They had never seen one before.
They all talked at once.

'UG UG!'

'OGGY OGGY ERF ERF!'

They tried eating the pencil.

YUK! YUK! YUK!

They even tried climbing the pencil.

WOAH!
That was no good.

The cavemen were stumped.

What was this thing for?

Then Colin
had a good
idea . . .

'OOF!' he said.

The other cavemen stopped to listen.

'MUGGA, HUGGA, LUGGA, RUGGA,' they said
when he had finished, and set straight to work.

Some carved.

Others chopped.

Suddenly Clive got excited.

'OOK, WEEL!' he said.
The others were very impressed.

At last it was finished.

Flint was excited too.

'BURNA BURNA
ROASTA TOASTA!'
he said.

But then . . .

. . . oh dear.
A very HUNGRY tiger appeared.

ROAAR

RR!

'OOK, CAR!'
shouted Carlos.

'MUGGA, HUGGA, LUGGA, RUGGA!'
said all the other cavemen.

And indeed, it was a very good idea!

They jumped into the car.
'GO-A, GO-A, GO-A!'

The car began to zoom off . . .

. . . straight over the fire.

'UGGA, PHEWA, NOTSO CHEWA!' said Colin.
And he was right – it had been a close one!

But the cavemen were so pleased with their great escape that they didn't see . . .

. . . the big tree.

'Oh, DUMMA
DUMMA,'
groaned Flint.

Then Colin
had another
good idea . . .

'OOF!' he said.

The other cavemen stopped to listen.

'MUGGA, HUGGA, LUGGA, RUGGA,' they said
when he had finished, and set straight to work.

Colin, Clive, Carlos and Flint got ready
at last for a tasty barbecue.

'YUM! YUM! YUM!'

Except . . .

... the tiger was back!

'OOK, no car!' said Carlos.

But he needn't have worried.
The tiger only wanted a sausage!
'UG-A-LUG!' said all the cavemen.

And indeed, it was a happy ending.